a day at the SEASHORE

By
Kathryn and Byron Jackson

Illustrated by Corinne Malvern

Nancy and Timmy hop out of their
beds as early as early can be.
  They put on their sunsuits—and
hurry downstairs—and eat breakfast
in one-two-and-three!

"What's in the basket?"
Good things to eat!

And the bag's full
of bathing suits, folded
and neat.

Now Nancy and Timmy are ready to go.
"Where?" barks the pup. He doesn't
know that you ride on a bus—

and you walk down a hill that smells sandy
and fresh—and then you stand still—
because down past the bath-houses,

down past the store that sells tin pails
and shovels, you can just see the shore.

A red pail for Nancy!
A blue pail for Tim!

And here is the place to get ready to swim.

You put on your bathing suit,
hang up your clothes,

and chuff through the sand. It feels hot to
your toes, just the way you remember from
coming before.

And, "Here you are, Puppy! You're down .
at the shore."

You can dig in the sand,
and build castles and dams.

You can catch little crabs—if you're quick!

You can draw great big pictures right on the beach with a piece of a shell or a stick.

You can wiggle your toes in the cool
little waves.

You can swim by yourself—if you're brave.

You can stay near the edge and hold tight to the rope, and get used to the splash of the sea.

You can watch all the ships that go sailing
away, till they dip down the sun-setting place.

You can hunt for a whale.

Or put shells in your pail.

Or throw sticks for
the puppy, or race.

And when Mother calls "Lunch time!"
you're hungry as bears.

"Bow wow!" barks the puppy. "A treat!"

And Nancy and Timmy sit down on the sand
and they eat
and they eat
and they EAT!